The Road Not Taken

Serendipity, Indiana - Book Six

by

Magdalena Scott

The Road Not Taken

© 2016 Magdalena Scott

ISBN-13: 978-0-9971922-6-1

Edited by Karen Block

Cover Art by Elusive Dreams Designs
Stock Art from DepositPhotos.com

Published by Jewel Box Books

DEDICATION

This book is dedicated to Susan Shields,
honorary citizen of Serendipity, Indiana.

ACKNOWLDGEMENTS

Among the items available for sale in Lillian Standish's Christmas Shop are CDs from "local musician Tom Rasely." He's not local to [the imaginary town of] Serendipity, but he is a real-life friend of mine, and his music has made my life better. Most particularly "Moonlight Concert," a collection of songs that lulled me to sleep many nights after my husband died. I thought Lillian might have listened to that CD too, after Harry's death, which happened prior to book one of this series.

As you can see, the people of Serendipity have become very real to me. I hope you'll come to care about them too.

Chapter One

BRAD TURNED THE car into the lane of the Christmas tree farm, and some of the stress built up during the long drive from Florida to Indiana fell away.

Home.

No matter how long I lived away from here, the peaceful feeling always settled over me when I returned to Serendipity.

From the placid scene of the hilly farm covered with evergreens and a thin skiff of snow, I dragged my eyes back to my husband. "Thank you again for making the trip, Brad. I know it's not your favorite place to spend the holidays."

He nodded, his eyes on the gravel lane. "You're welcome, again, Francie. Where else am I going to spend Christmas than with my son and wife?"

That sounded simple, but he and I both knew better. Our marriage was in trouble. I wasn't sure how or when it had begun to deteriorate, but I feared this was our last Christmas together, unless something drastic happened to turn things around.

Heading up the driveway, we passed my sister Carla's house on the right. On the left was the small acreage my parents gave me when I turned twenty-one. Unlike Carla and our brothers Jim and David, I had never built my dream home here. Had never lived the life as an adult that looked so idyllic—residing on a Christmas tree farm, selling trees and working in the Christmas shop during the holidays.

It was hard work much of the year, but because we worked together and our family was close-knit, the effort was always worthwhile. Time spent with customers in the Christmas shop was the easy part— more like play than work to me, with the CDs providing holiday music, families shopping together… Okay, sometimes that part was stressful to endure, depending on how well the kids and adults behaved.

After Dad died, every facet of the farm business

changed. At first, my brother Jim had tried to shoulder all of Dad's responsibilities, but he eventually had to hire help so he could keep his law practice going. Mom, who had always been in charge of the Christmas shop, helped Jim in overseeing the farm's operations. She also ran the relatively new sideline—the tiny cabin B&B. I leaned my forehead on the cool glass of the passenger side window, feeling anew our family's loss.

Brad parked the Prius in front of the house I'd grown up in, as close to the edge of the gravel pad as possible, since the parking area is also used by customers who come to cut their own trees and peruse the shop.

Mom appeared on the front porch, her dog Daisy at her side. Daisy had been Dad's, but after his death, she became Mom's near constant companion. I tore out of the car and ran up onto the porch, and Mom enveloped me in a hug.

"Sweetheart, I'm so glad you're here." She held me, rubbing my back as if I were a small child. I had to steel myself to keep from crying. At last I found my voice and pulled back a little.

"It's great to be here, Mom. Thanks for putting up with our last-minute decision."

Brad walked up the wooden porch steps and set down the first load of luggage. He moved toward Mom and I took a step away. He hugged her briefly and kissed her cheek. "What Francie said, Lillian. I'm embarrassed that we called you so late to see if you have room."

"Have room? My goodness, of course I have room for my baby daughter and favorite son-in-law."

The thought flashed into my head to wonder if she would call Jared Barnett *favorite son-in-law* once he and Carla got married. By that time, it was possible Brad and I would be divorced. My breath caught, anticipating the conversation we would need to have with Joseph, and with my family. Like the proverbial elephant in the room, the breakdown of our relationship in the last few years had been something neither of us wanted to talk about—even keeping it between the two people who might be able to repair the situation. In all the hours of our drive north, we had studiously avoided discussing anything personal. During my stints at driving, there was no conversation at all. Brad was too focused on his phone or laptop to talk.

Mom's cheerful voice broke into my depressing reverie. "If I had known ahead of time that you were coming, I wouldn't have begun the renovations upstairs. You don't mind staying in one of the cabins, do you?"

Brad's jaw dropped, and I can only assume mine did too. He recovered more quickly though. "No room at the inn, as they say." He turned to me, one eyebrow cocked. "We can be flexible, can't we, Francie?"

"Um. Sure. Sure, that's not a problem." I hadn't spent much time in any of the cabins that were part of the farm's bed and breakfast business, but from what I remembered, they were truly *tiny*. Was there enough space for two people who used to be intimate life partners but no longer were?

Mom sighed with relief. "Oh, good. I'm so glad you don't mind. Do you want to see what's going on with the rooms upstairs?"

We abandoned our bags and followed Mom

through the living room and up the stairs to the bedroom Carla and I used to share. Mom opened the door.

Most of the wallpaper had been scraped off, but stubborn layers of old paper remained in patches here and there. The woodwork had been scraped too. Paint chips in a variety of colors littered the floor. The posters and other teenage memorabilia were long gone, no doubt. Most of all, the twin beds were missing.

"Oh. My. Word." I couldn't help it, and lucky for all of us, I hadn't let loose with something more colorful.

Mom put an arm around my shoulders. "It's just a start, you know. When we're done here, the room will be fit for royalty. You'll love it." She squeezed me and let go, stepping further into the room.

I staggered after her.

Mom looked thrilled with the renovation, and I didn't dare say what I was really thinking. "Wow. This is a surprise. I guess I was picturing new curtains, maybe some paint."

Brad remained in the hallway, taking in the

devastation of the room where he and I always stayed when visiting. "Whoa. It's major, Lillian."

She hurried on, unaware of our shock. "It was time, I'd say. I had lots of help deciding which way to go, as you can imagine. Carla, and Jared's daughter Katie, both had ideas about everything. Katie's very creative. She's promised to help me with the sewing, since Carla is so busy at her dress shop. Katie is learning to machine embroider too. She's trying out her new skill on the coverlet and matching curtains. But, you know, at fourteen, she has lots going on at school and extracurricular events."

"That's nice," I muttered.

Her face fell, and not wanting to hurt her feelings, I pasted a smile on mine. Something was different with Mom today, but I wasn't sure what.

"Don't get me wrong. I'm sure it'll be nice. I'm just surprised."

"There didn't seem to be any reason to leave it as a museum to you and Carla when you've had your own homes all these years. That's why I sent you the boxes of things from the closet, remember? I found a few other items in the attic too. They should fit into your trunk for the return trip. Carla took the beds to put in the room that will be Katie's whenever Jared and Carla finally tie the knot. You remember I asked if you wanted any of the furniture, right, Francie?" Her voice was filled with concern about my reaction to the room.

"Yes. Yes, I remember, and that's totally fine. And—let me think—you're going to rent this room out as part of the B&B?"

"Well, that's a possibility. Jim and David are against the idea. Those boys are overprotective of me and insist the B&B guests only belong in the tiny cabins. I think if it were up to them, I wouldn't serve breakfast during tree season at all."

"Why's that, Lillian?" Brad was leaning against the doorframe, handsome and casual—not flipping out as I felt myself doing.

Mom scraped with her thumbnail at a piece of wallpaper that refused to budge. "Because there isn't a way to serve them in the Christmas shop during tree season, and I host breakfast in my dining room instead. I figure it gets the good china out of the cabinet one month each year. Really, it's easier to have them in the dining room than to carry everything to the shop building across the parking area. But Jim and David don't understand that part."

"What's their room like?" I blurted out.

"Their room? Oh, the boys' old room. Come and see." We followed her across the hall. The bedroom David and Jim had shared was always a boys-only territory which historically housed a variety of creepy pets, concert posters, and their sports trophies.

We strolled through the large bedroom, noting a variety of stuffed Santa figures, Nativity sets, and a big plastic Rudolph suspended from the ceiling smiling down at us.

Brad chuckled, shaking his head. "Wow. Salute to Christmas, huh?"

Mom nodded. "Pretty much. Can anyone guess who worked with me on the plan for this room?"

Our son Joseph appeared from the hall, strode to each of us in turn and administered bone-crushing hugs. "Hey, guys. What do you think of my room? Grandma said since I'm the one who stays here the most, I could decide what it looks like."

Evidently, our recent college grad was more of a Christmas junkie than either of us realized.

"It's… It's very Christmassy." That was all I had. What it was, in my opinion, was overdone to a massive degree. "How much of this glows in the dark?"

Joseph bounded over onto the messily pulled-together bed. "Not that much. And I sleep with my eyes closed anyway. Only thing I miss from the way it used to be is the bunk beds, but Matthew has those now, which is awesome."

Mom crooked her finger. "Let's go downstairs and I'll get you something to eat. Do you need a nap before dinner?" She was leading the way down the steps not watching the reaction from Brad or me.

Thank goodness.

Chapter Two

MOM SET OUT a plate of homemade cookies, poured milk into glasses for me and Joseph, and made a fresh pot of coffee for Brad. She continued to chatter about her redecorating project while she bustled around. "The main expense is the mattress sets. Reba and I haunted antique auctions for a few weeks and bought the furniture for almost nothing. It's such a shame how little interest there is in high quality pieces like the ones I bought."

Reba Markland and Mom have been friends since The Year One. They threw us kids and Reba's kids together for holidays or any other potential event. I'm sure—almost—that the two of them didn't push my brother David into a romance with Reba's granddaughter Emily. But if they did, we'd forgive them. David and Emily have a happy marriage and are expecting their first child. Another grandchild for Mom and Reba's first great-grand.

"How's Emily?" I asked around a chocolate chip cookie. "Will she be here today?"

"Emily's doing well. Just five months to go. And everyone but Carla will be here this evening." Mom consulted her watch. "In a couple of hours, in fact. We've had a busy season so far. You can imagine, Francie, how much traffic there was on the evening we got that speck of snow that's still trying to hold on."

I laughed and glanced at Brad to see how bored he was with the discussion. "I'm sure it was a southern Indiana madhouse. The idea of chopping down the family Christmas tree during a snowstorm, or even a light snow flurry, is a big deal to everybody but us."

"It sure is a big deal," Joseph said, smiling from me to Brad and back again. "This farm is holiday cheer central. After a year of bad news from everywhere, people *need* good, old-fashioned traditions. Places like this are reassuring just because we're friendly, family owned, and low tech. Maybe they get some hope for the future by connecting to the past during the Christmas season."

"You might be getting a little carried away, son," Brad said, winking. "Been dipping into the eggnog?"

"No, I'm serious. We've had a lot of customers this year who have never cut their own tree before. It's a huge deal for them to drive here, bring the kids, tromp all over the farm until the big spotlight seems to beam on their perfect tree. Then they hack it down. There's gonna be a lot of work cleaning up jagged stumps next spring." He shook his head. "Like I said, we've seen a lot of customers who've never cut a tree before or even held a saw."

"There's always a lot of cleanup." I remembered going out with Dad to do such things. It was just part of growing up on the farm.

Mom walked over to a pegboard near the backdoor and returned with a key. "This is for cabin five. It overlooks the lake—such a lovely spot. You won't have trouble finding it, will you?"

I held out my hand, and she dropped the key

into it. "Guess not, unless you moved the lake."

Brad pushed his chair back and stood. "Well then. Shall we take our bags back to the car and drive up to our home-away-from-home?"

Mom grinned up at him.

Joseph got up and shrugged into his coat. "See you guys later at the Christmas shop."

As soon as Brad started the Prius, I sent a text to Carla asking if she had room for us in her house. I found it irritating Brad was being pleasant when in the presence of Mom and Joseph about this change in plan. I waited for the snide comments I knew he was all too eager to vent. It's not as if my husband and I wanted to be jammed up together in a miniature cabin for two weeks.

****

Almost as soon as I sent the text, Carla called me.

"Hey, welcome home, Francie! You know I'd love to have you guys stay with me, but no-can-do this year. I've got sewing projects from the shop stashed everywhere, plus I have some rooms in the process of redecoration for Katie and Miles. My hours are horrible, so even if I had space, no one would get a decent night's sleep staying with me. I thought Mom said she had some cabins available."

"Yes, she does. We're headed up to one right now. I just thought, you know, it might give us more time to chat if we stayed with you. But no problem, Carla. I'll stop in at the shop to see you. Is that the best way to be sure of an audience with the great and powerful dress designer?"

"Ha. Don't make fun of me. I swear this Christmas season is busier than ever. The whole year has been busier than ever. If not for some excellent help and a fiancée who knows how to give great neck rubs, I'd be hospitalized by now."

"Well, I'm glad you've got good people on your side, Carla. I'll be in to see you as soon as I can." I closed the connection and dropped my phone back in my purse.

Brad was maneuvering the gravel track toward the lake. "I take it her answer was no."

"That's the short version."

We rounded the last corner and the cabin came into view. Brad pulled up next to it and shut off the engine. "Unless you have another plan, we might just as well take our bags in here and get settled."

The door unlocked easily, and we entered from the miniature front porch that sported two red-painted rocking chairs. I dropped my tote bag onto one of the two easy chairs next to a small electric wall unit that looked too teensy to heat even an abode for Barbie. A baby cedar tree wrapped in fairy lights sat in a pot on the windowsill.

For newlyweds, maybe it was ideal. For Brad and me, not so much. Although we still shared a bed at home, it was a king size with plenty of space to *not* touch each other. Sometimes Brad's snoring, or my tossing and turning, resulted in one of us spending the night in the guest room. How long would it be until one of us moved to the guest room permanently...until the word *divorce* was mentioned? It felt inevitable.

I looked around and almost wished we had stayed home. "Oh man. Can you believe people pay money to spend time in these doll houses?"

Following me under the mistletoe we were both ignoring, Brad walked through the *living room* in two strides and put a hand on the ladder. It rolled easily from one side of the room to the other, making built-in cabinetry, bookshelves, and the walkway to the back of the space more accessible. He climbed up two or three rungs and peeked at the loft area. "Didn't you say Emily spent some time in one of these before she married David?"

"Yes, she did. But she's only one person." I was in no hurry to see what was supposed to be a bedroom. I eyed the two chairs. If there'd been three, I might have managed to remove the seat cushions and create a little bed for myself, as backup in case the upstairs was too...cozy. I tried a cushion but it was fastened tight. Resigned, I poked around the kitchen.

The mini fridge was empty, as expected, but a variety of teabags resided in a handmade basket on the countertop. I put the kettle on and fussed with the tea things until the water boiled. "Jared stayed in one of the cabins with Miles and Katie a couple of years ago too.

I'm sure we can make this work. It's just not ideal."

Actually, I wasn't sure at all that we could co-exist here without our problems flaring out of control. But maybe that's what we needed. For a long time we had lived under the same roof, behaving as near strangers. Here, that wouldn't be an option. Either we worked out our problems or one of us would leave.

Chapter Three

I SPENT THE evening working in the Christmas shop. As usual, Mom had the place well stocked with homemade items like cookies and wassail mix, Christmas decor of all sorts, and holiday music CDs including one by local musician Tom Rasely. Most everyone who bought a tree also ended up with something from the Christmas shop, even if it was just a free cup of hot cocoa or wassail.

"I'm glad you decided to come up for the holiday," Emily said when a family exited the shop and we had a couple of quieter moments. "Joseph sure seems to love it here. He's been marvelous help to Jim and David. Jim had already planned on hiring a couple of local young men to help too—guys he knows who need the work. Since Joseph is pitching in, everyone gets a day off each week."

"That's a big deal," I said. "We never used to get any time off during tree season."

She nodded. "So David has mentioned. One of those love-hate things, where he looked forward to his month-off-the-day-job to work here and grow his annual beard, yet he knew he'd be more tired after Christmas than at any other time of the year."

I watched her eyes sparkle as she talked about her husband. "Lucky David. Thank goodness he found you to take care of him. To be honest, I expected him to be a lifelong bachelor. Working all week and coming home on the weekends to live on the backside of the farm wasn't exactly a great way to meet Ms. Right. Or so it seemed until you grew up and changed his boring little life. Is my brother still the consummate slob?"

She grimaced. "Sorry to say that hasn't changed at all. I hope our baby doesn't take after him in the neatness department, or I'll never again have a house I can allow a visitor to step into."

I wrapped an arm around her shoulders, not wanting to crowd the growing baby bump. "I hope the

Kincaid-Standish youngster will be just like you, Emily."

She blushed. "Thanks, Francie. What a sweet thing to say."

The door burst open and my eight-year-old nephew Matthew ran in. "Hey, Aunt Francie! I saw Uncle Brad and he said you need a hug." He squeezed me around the middle.

"Thanks for the awesome greeting, Matthew." I sank into a chair so we were nearer the same height. "Are you working in here with us?"

He rolled his eyes and dropped the volume of his voice. "I wanna work outside helping give out the saws and tying down trees on top of cars. But my dad says I'm still too little." He glanced at Mom who was giving out a free cup of cocoa and discussing cookie recipes. "I love Grandma and everything, but being the only boy in here is... Well, sorry, but it's boring."

I clamped a hand over my mouth to keep from laughing out loud at his heartrending little-boy angst. That's when his mother Melissa walked in. Matthew excused himself and hurried to the small desk Mom had created for him that first Christmas he was with us.

"Mel!" Another big hug and another release of stress. Melissa has been a close friend to both Carla and me all our lives. The whole family was relieved when Jim finally figured out he had a second chance at love with his high school girlfriend. Having Melissa and Matthew in our family changed all of us for the better.

She took a hard look at me and shook her head at what she saw. "Francie, I'm scheming to get some girl time for the four of us. It's been way too long. Alice and Robert will get to town in a couple of days. They're staying with Alice's folks, of course. Getting Carla out of her shop for even a few hours may be the biggest problem. I've asked why she doesn't just set up a cot in the workroom. She's pulling some super long days, and that's without any projects from me." Melissa smiled and I knew what she was remembering.

But then again didn't we all smile—or perhaps cringe—at the memory of the crazy December in which Mel and Jim's wedding was thrown together between the first and twenty-fifth? Carla, on the other hand, might like to block the memory, since she had done most of the work on the bridal and attendant gowns.

I picked up a sock monkey that sported a Santa hat. "I got that idea when I talked to her this afternoon. I guess she isn't able to work here in the shop at all anymore. That's a shame."

"Your mom told her we had plenty of help, which we do. I think Lillian worries about Carla."

"You know it's a mom thing. She worries about all of us."

Mel tipped her head, one brow arched as she looked at me. I heard her unspoken statement loud and clear—*She's worried about you, Francie.*

"I'm fine, Mel. Really."

She gave me a hug and whispered, "Liar," then was off to help a customer choose the right type of lights for his front porch.

****

The next morning Brad, Joseph and I drank coffee in the kitchen while Mom served a breakfast casserole to the other tiny cabin B&B customers.

Joseph looked through the cereal choices in the

cabinet. "What the B&B peeps are having smells good. I like to wait and see if there are any leftovers."

I found a box of plain oat cereal, cut up a banana on top of it, and searched without results for some walnuts. "If I eat a huge hunk of casserole I'll be ready for a nap," I said. "Brad? Cereal or casserole?"

Brad looked up from his phone, frowning. "What? Oh, nothing for me. I'm good with coffee. I'm going to drive into town soon, and can pick up a doughnut there." His gaze went back to the phone.

My eyes met Joseph's across the table. Brad was more distant and less communicative all the time. It was one thing for him to behave that way when it was just me, but we didn't see Joseph often and should be making the most of our time with him.

I poured myself another cup of coffee and topped off Brad's too. "Do you mind if I ride into town with you? I'd like to drop in on Carla."

Brad checked his watch. "Oh. Sure, come along. I'd like to leave in fifteen minutes."

I downed a slug of coffee and regretted the large helping of cereal I had prepared. "I'll be ready."

Joseph cleared his throat. "Dad, are you reading the *Wall Street Journal* or something on your phone? When I was at home, you'd have taken mine away from me if I did that at the table."

Brad looked up at our son, his frown deepening. "It's work, okay?"

I felt myself shrink into the chair. Was it work? Did I even want to know why he spent so much time online? Brad was on that phone or his laptop all the time, and even last night as we lay as far apart as we could on the queen-size mattress on the floor of the cabin's loft, the light of my husband's phone made me cover my head with the comforter instead of looking up at the stars through the skylight. I guess I was asleep by the time he shut the thing off.

I invited Joseph to come with us but he didn't have errands in town and preferred to stay at the farm and do any tasks Mom assigned. I could tell she loved having him around and that the feeling was mutual. I was so proud of Joseph. How many young men would leave Denver for two weeks to work on a family Christmas tree farm in Nowhere, Indiana?

At least our years of marriage weren't a total loss. We had created a wonderful young man who cared deeply about others. And thank goodness, Joseph wasn't following in his father's footsteps of being consumed by his career.

****

I looked over at Brad as he slowed at the city limits. Neither of us had spoken during the short drive into town. "I'm surprised at Joseph's choice to spend the holiday here. Especially since we never made a point of coming to Serendipity for Christmas when he was young." I'd always wanted to, but Brad insisted we needed to make our own family traditions, instead of relying on what he always referred to as *extended* family.

Brad turned left onto High Street. "Same here. When I was his age, this isn't the location I would have chosen."

"That's certainly true," I said, immediately regretting the combative tone.

He let out a long breath. "We're here now,

okay? Can that be good enough for the moment, Francie?"

"Sure thing," I muttered. He stopped at the intersection with Market Street. "I'll just get out here and walk to Carla's shop. Where and when should we meet?" I opened my door.

"I'll send you a text when I'm ready to go. That work?"

"I guess." I got out and closed the door, and without looking back, started toward the town square. What reason did Brad have to come into town today? Maybe he just wanted to get away from me and my family for a while since Joseph was busy with tasks at the farm. I shook my head to clear some of the negative thoughts out of it. No reason to saddle Carla with anything but good cheer. From what I'd heard of her workload, she didn't need more complications.

****

When the bell over the door jingled, a pleasant-faced, middle-aged woman greeted me.

"Well, good morning, Francie. You probably

don't remember me from junior high days."

"Oh, of course I do, Mrs. Glass. Carla has told me what a huge help you are to her."

When an overload of projects had pressed Carla too hard, she hit on the idea of hiring the woman who had taught sewing to us and hundreds of others when she was a home economics teacher at Serendipity Junior High. State standards had strangely resulted in the removal of the program that taught young people how to sew, cook, and run a home—which left Mrs. Glass unemployed.

The older woman blushed. I wasn't certain I'd ever seen her smile when I was her student, let alone blush. "I love working here with Carla. Did she tell you about the evening sewing classes? I'm taking those over for the most part. You might imagine Katie Barnett is one of my best students."

"That doesn't surprise me at all." Katie's dad was Carla's fiancée, and I knew her slightly. She was extremely creative and always had projects underway.

"Let me get Carla for you," Mrs. Glass offered. "She finally learned she doesn't have to hop up and leave a project when the bell jingles now that I'm here."

I took a moment to look at the beautiful items on display as well as professional, life-size photos of some of Carla's famous designs. Sometimes I found it hard to believe I have a sister who makes dresses worn on the red carpet at the Academy Awards and other high profile events.

"Hey, Sis." Carla flowed into the showroom looking as glamorous as the famous women depicted on her walls. Her eyes and skin were glowing, although dark circles under her eyes hinted at her lack of sleep.

I held her at arm's length for a moment. "Carla, I've never seen you look happier. It's obvious love agrees with you."

"Well, there you go. I can thank you, Mel, and Alice for helping push me and Jared together. Even though I don't think any of you believed I'd stay in a relationship with a man who had kids."

I shrugged. "We can't be right about everything. Just *almost* everything. I'm thrilled for you, honey." And part of me was just the teensiest bit jealous. "Will you have any time away from the shop before

December twenty-fifth? I think Mel's considering an intervention while Alice is in town to get you away from work for at least a few hours."

Carla's smile was tired. "I'll do what I can. Irene—you know, Mrs. Glass—can hold down the fort for a while. But whatever I don't accomplish during the workday I have to make up for at night. Just like Dad always told us, people think having your own business means *less* work, when it really means *more.*"

"I do remember him saying that, and we sure worked our tails off a lot of the time, didn't we? I guess growing up on the farm taught us all how important it is to always do our best. Okay. About the girlfriend time—we'll see what we can figure out, short of carrying you from the shop, bound and gagged. That would make dinner at the *Barbeque Basement* entertaining for us but awkward for you."

The door opened and two women came in. They looked almost familiar but, thank goodness, they didn't embarrass us all with *I bet you don't remember me,* because they'd be right. I'd been gone from Serendipity so long I'd forgotten names of most mere acquaintances. Irene swept over to hear their concerns about whether their special order would be ready on the scheduled day. Carla's eyes rolled. She gave me a quick, light hug and whispered, "Talk later, Francie. So glad you're home!"

Chapter Four

I TOOK MY time walking around the town square. I was sad to see several empty store fronts. Jared Barnett had been hired to lead the economic development office for the county. I didn't know him well, but he was smart and energetic, and since he had chosen to raise his children in Serendipity, he would have the best interest of the community at heart. It had to be a good thing to have new ideas flowing for a change. Serendipity needed more employment for its citizens if it was to stem problems like drugs, theft, and other issues associated with hopelessness.

I stopped in at *Emily's Dreams*, the consignment store my sister-in-law had started, but which was now owned by her aunt, Darlene Kincaid. As in Carla's shop, a bell over the door announced my presence.

Jennifer Kincaid, Emily's mom, appeared from the side room.

"Well, Francie. It's great to see you!" She hugged me. "Emily said you had decided to spend a few days here. What fun for everyone."

Everyone but Brad—and me when I was with Brad—but oh well.

"I love being home at Christmas. How are you doing, Jennifer?"

She dimpled. "Terrific. I'm going to be a grandma, for goodness sake! How can that even be?"

"I don't know. Seems impossible that any of us are over eighteen. Emily looks fabulous, and it's wonderful to be anticipating a new life." I looked around the display area. "So, are you enjoying the store?"

She gestured at the neatly organized space. "Yes, it's fun to have this little place to run. Keeps me off the street and out of trouble. Ben won't be home for Christmas this year. He's on the west coast, you know. The girls are in town though. Taylor and Hannah are seniors at Indiana University, Bloomington campus. It's just surreal to me that they're all grown up. I'm trying to get ready for the possibility the girls will find jobs far away, like Ben. Most of the time Marcus and I rattle around in the house. Not that I'm necessarily complaining." She winked, and it was obvious that their marriage was doing just fine.

"Try to think of their new homes as vacation destinations," I suggested, steering my mind from marriages back to kids. "My son Joseph is in Colorado, which is quite a haul from Florida. But I visit him every two or three months. He's busy, but finds time to show me around a little bit. When he's working, I explore on my own. I enjoy it." Brad seldom went with me on these trips. More and more, his work was his life.

She nodded, unconvinced. "That's what Marcus says, and then I point out we don't have money to travel after putting three kids through college." She laughed. "I can't complain. We're all happy and healthy. Emily said your Joseph is doing a lot for Lillian. Mother has been so impressed with him. I think he helped lug a bunch of antiques up the stairs after your mother and mine bought a load of stuff at some auctions."

"I'm glad Joseph is such a part of the holiday this year. It's a surprise to me, Jennifer, since we didn't bring him here for Christmas when he was little."

"It's interesting, isn't it, when our children grow up and make their own decisions? My goodness, after Emily had her car wreck, she became a different person. Different in a good way—for her and for us. But still, it was something to get used to."

But Joseph hadn't had a life-changing experience like a car wreck. What he did have was a set of parents whose relationship was disintegrating. Maybe his philosophical statement when Mom was giving us the cabin key—that customers get some hope for the future by connecting to the past during the Christmas season—hadn't been just about customers. Perhaps because of Brad and me, Joseph needed to return to this simpler lifestyle for a time to rejuvenate himself.

Jennifer looked at me quizzically. "Francie? Are you okay?"

"Oh. Yes, I'm fine. Sorry I checked out for a minute. Something just occurred to me."

A few minutes later I was on the sidewalk again, absently looking in shop windows. Maybe I was wrong about Joseph's reason for being at the farm. Brad and I hadn't said anything to our son about having marital problems. Even when my friends or family were concerned that something was wrong with us, I refused to go into it. Either he and I would fix our marriage or we would not, but letting others into the situation could only complicate it, not help.

Had we protected Joseph from hurt by not talking to him about our problems? Or had we done the opposite?

I texted Brad to pick me up at the same place he dropped me. It was fifteen minutes or so before he arrived. As soon as he pulled up at the stop sign, I was off the curb and inside the car. "Where were you? It's freezing outside. Couldn't you have let me know when you'd be here?"

"Why did you want me to pick you up on a corner that has no protection from the weather? Why not wait in Carla's shop?"

I held my hands by the heater, trying to thaw

them. "I didn't want to bother her."

"Standing inside her store is a bother?"

"She's busy." Of course I could have waited in her shop. There was no reason to blame Brad for my choice, but this sniping-for-no-reason was typical for us now.

Brad let out a slow breath. "I'm sure she's busy. Francie, I don't want to argue about this. You're in the car now." Resignation colored his voice. "Other stops or just back to the farm?"

I dug my phone out of my purse again. "I should have asked if Mom needs anything from the grocery. Let me call her."

Brad pulled into a parking space and beat an impatient rhythm on the steering wheel while I talked to Mom. I ended the call and dropped the phone back where it had been. "She's good. We could stop at *Something Sweet*, though—"

"Check the backseat. I've done the bakery. One dozen assorted, plus half a dozen walnut brownies."

The telltale white box and small white sack sat on the backseat, and the sweet smell was apparent to me now. "Okay. That's great." He'd gotten our usual order. We always set the box on Mom and Dad's kitchen table, and whoever came through during the next day or two took what they wanted.

After a couple decades of marriage, there are some things Brad and I understood about each other. But in the last few years, the misunderstandings had become more frequent. He was more dedicated to his career than he was to his marriage, though he'd never admit it. And in spite of myself, I was increasingly bitter.

The deafening silence was back. "So, what did you find to do in Serendipity besides the bakery trip?"

Brad shrugged, a sign that he wasn't going to give me a direct answer. "Not much. Drove around town. With the empty storefronts around the square and noticeable lack of maintenance on homes, it doesn't look very prosperous."

"Jared just started as economic development director. Maybe things will turn around. I'm sure it won't be quick though." Truth be told, Carla's husband-to-be might have a bigger challenge getting the community to consider new ways of looking at its future than he would in finding businesses interested in locating in the area.

"Nothing happens fast around here, does it?" Brad asked.

I could see Serendipity's faults but having them pointed out to me was aggravating. "I realize you don't want to be here. You have *never* wanted to be here. But please don't feel that you have to enumerate everything that's wrong with my hometown."

I looked out the window. We'd had this same conversation countless times. Brad could never seem to appreciate any facets of the community. Today I wasn't in the mood to list them for him. Sometimes I wondered what had attracted him to me when he met me at college, since I'd spilled my entire history the first time we spoke that day in a deserted classroom. He knew from the start that I was from a small, quiet town.

In my mind I ran through some of the pluses of Serendipity. In short, the little place has a big heart. The fact that it doesn't have large dollar signs or high profile cases spelled D-U-L-L to Brad. Why couldn't he see that a shiny name plate on the office door, and ever-growing numbers on the investment reports, don't always equate with a happy life?

Chapter Five

JOSEPH WAS PREPARING dinner for us in Mom's kitchen.

"This is a special treat," Mom said, sitting quietly at the kitchen table. It was a sight I hadn't witnessed many times—someone else working in that room while Mom kicked back and relaxed. She looked happy, but that *something else* was evident again. I'd need to get her alone and see if she would open up to me. No one else mentioned anything unusual going on with Mom, yet I was certain I wasn't imagining it.

I asked to help, and Joseph pointed to a pile of washed potatoes ready to be peeled.

"I like to cook," Joseph said. "Plus it's a treat for me to get a bunch of the family together as often as possible while I'm here. Once I leave, I'm on my own again, back to the boring bachelor life."

"I'm sure the bachelor life isn't as dull as all that," I said, picking up a potato.

He smiled. "It's okay."

"But you haven't found that one certain girl yet?"

Mom shot me a warning glance.

Joseph didn't look up. "I'm not looking for a long-term relationship."

I paused in mid-peel. "Well, but, honey, when the right girl comes along—"

"Grandma, how's the Christmas shop doing?" I blushed at Joseph's obvious change of subject. It couldn't have been more obvious he didn't want me prying in his personal life if he had said, *Mind your own business.*

Mom didn't look relaxed and happy anymore, but sad. I felt that way too. I wasn't trying to push Joseph into marriage right away, but he should at least be open to the possibility of finding a life partner. Just because his parents' marriage wasn't working didn't mean that his wouldn't.

While we chopped and peeled, Mom told a few

funny stories of things that had happened in the shop this year. Emily came in the back door and shrugged off her coat in the mudroom. She was glowing.

"Thanks for the text about dinner, Joseph. I'm starved, as usual. I could have eaten a meal every time I finished one of the cabins today." She smiled, blushing a little. I guess she was embarrassed at her increased appetite.

"How many of the cabins are occupied now?" I asked. I didn't understand small families choosing to spend time in those miniscule spaces at any time of year, let alone the week before Christmas. Brad and I both found the confinement in that tiny space to be unnerving and couldn't wait to get out of the cabin each morning and go our separate ways.

"Six, but after tomorrow, we're down to four. I think it's cool two families are staying through December twenty-sixth. Plus you guys." Emily broke a doughnut in half and closed the lid on the box. "Francie, did you know we got a write-up in the travel magazine for southern Indiana?"

"Umm. I don't remember hearing that, but it's

great advertising, I bet."

"Sure is. We have lots of different types of promotion, but the best is word of mouth. Loads of guests say they heard about us from friends who've stayed here. We were totally booked several weekends this summer."

A thought occurred to me. "What about breakfast for the guests on Christmas morning?"

Mom took plates out of the cupboard and started setting the table. "I told those folks when they booked, that Christmas morning breakfast would be delivered to them, instead of served here. I'll be making a casserole for us anyway, and it's not a problem to deliver some to those two cabins. It all works out, Francie, if you're open to new possibilities."

Was she talking about more than breakfast? How much did Mom guess about what was going on with Brad and me? She'd never pressed me for information, although Mel and the girls had tried to get me to open up more than once.

I finished peeling the last potato and got out of Joseph's way. "I'd like to hear more about the day-today running of the farm and the cabins, Mom. I know things have changed a lot in recent years."

"Work on the farm itself hasn't changed so much, but the B&B lends its own interesting twist to the day. I'm thankful for it though. So glad Mel suggested the idea."

"I love working with the B&B," Emily said. "Anything you want to know, just ask." She paused like she had been hit with a bolt of insight. "In fact, do you want to come along with me tomorrow when I do my cabin visit routine?"

Thank goodness. An opportunity to make myself useful during the day. "I'd love to, Emily. Thanks."

David appeared from the mudroom, his holiday beard looking a bit scruffier than yesterday. I hadn't even heard him come in. "You'll be learning from the best, Francie. Emily's awesome at everything she does." Love glowed in his eyes, and I was thankful, again, that he and Emily had found each other. Brad and I had been that way at one time. What had changed us? It wasn't just the years; Mom and Dad had been married for over forty years and never lost the spark. On the other hand, ours had been sputtering for some time now.

Mom put her arm around Emily's thickening waist. "Yes, Emily's wonderful help. I just want you both to remember the decision of when you come back to work after the baby is born is up to you. Do *not* make the choice based on what you think *I* need. If Emily wants to stay home and be a full-time mommy for a while, I'll find someone to step in temporarily. If a few months turn into a few years, that's fine too. Everything will work out."

Emily kissed Mom's cheek. "Thanks, Lillian. I appreciate your attitude. David and I both do." She looked at me. "Your mom is the best boss I've ever had, Francie."

I helped myself to the other half of the doughnut Emily had broken off. "I can imagine."

I didn't want to ask now, in case Mom was just blowing smoke for David and Emily's sake, but I did wonder if she had anyone in mind. No way did I want Mom taking on more than she could handle. Active as she was, her age would eventually catch up with her. Maybe I should find a way to have a private chat with Jim since he was overseeing the farm, employees who worked with the trees, and other behind-the-scenes tasks Dad had always done.

My heart broke again at the loss of our father. His absence continued to impact daily life here. It wasn't easier to mourn him from Florida, just different. For some reason, being on the farm brought a renewed connection to his memory.

Joseph served roast beef, carrots and potatoes, and what he called *cheating* rolls because they were from the grocery's freezer. I was thankful he had thought of making dinner. Otherwise everyone would have grabbed fast food or eaten leftovers at their own houses, instead of having this together time.

We sat in the dining room, unlike the days when growing up here, the four of us kids and our parents fit around the kitchen table. Now a weekly Sunday lunch at the dining table had become routine, but I hadn't been around when that happened.

Just as the food was being passed, we heard

Carla's Mustang pull up out front. She arrived slightly breathless, her cheeks pink from the cold wind that picked up earlier in the afternoon. She dropped into a chair next to Joseph, after giving him a hug. "You're a lifesaver, you know. If not for your kind invitation, I'd still be at the shop with no hope of a decent meal." She took a deep breath and visibly seemed to shed the day's stress. "I'm sorry Jared and the kids couldn't be here with me. They're in Indianapolis for a few days. He's attending some meetings, and Katie and Miles are spending time with their grandparents. There's still no love lost between the Peabodys and Jared, yet he makes certain that the kids frequently see their deceased mother's parents."

I smoothed the napkin in my lap. "Carla, hold out your hand. I've seen your engagement ring as a tiny picture on my phone, but we were rushed the other day and I forgot to ask."

She held up her left hand, and the small solitaire diamond of our Grandma Standish's engagement ring caught the light and sparkled blue.

"It's beautiful, honey." I'd been so young at the

time Carla lost the ring that I didn't remember it at all. I barely remembered Grandma Standish, and maybe the "memories" were really the result of looking at photographs and hearing stories.

She looked down at the ring. "I know. I couldn't have wanted anything prettier. But I had given up ever seeing it again."

"Things happen the way they're supposed to," Mom said, and everyone agreed. The miracle of that ring reappearing when it did still amazed me.

I felt mean-spirited to be jealous of Carla's bit of magic that had been all the sign she needed to convince her she and Jared Barnett were meant for each other. Thank goodness, the magic worked, since he had been ready to propose.

Mel and Jim, David and Emily, and our friend Alice and her now-husband Robert had all experienced their own magic. As far as I knew, their relationships were marvelous. Brad and I had been married for a long time, much of it happily, but no magic had ever sprinkled us with fairy dust. Had I made a mistake marrying him without it?

But no—that couldn't be right, because if there'd been no Brad, there would be no Joseph. And our son Joseph was, I often reminded myself, our gift to the future.

Brad had even less than usual to say at dinner. Why couldn't he try harder to get along with my family? He and Jim seemed especially cold to each other on this visit. Had Jim picked up on what was going on with Brad and me? Ever the big brother, he might have stepped in and spoken to Brad on my behalf. I knew that could only make things worse.

When we'd eaten almost everything, Joseph brought a fruit salad into the dining room. "I don't want to hear complaints about dessert. We've all been eating doughnuts, right?"

Matthew perked up. "Doughnuts?"

Mel mouthed a *Thanks a lot* at Joseph. I smiled remembering how I'd tried to control Joseph's food choices when he was that age.

Before anyone could kick back and start reminiscing, another vehicle pulled into the gravel parking area.

Matthew hurried to the window. "Customer!"

Everyone went into action. Jim and David pulled on their coats and headed out to man the station with maps of the farm and handsaws for those who didn't bring their own. Mom hugged Joseph and thanked him again for dinner, and she, Emily, and Mel bundled up before walking across the parking area to open the Christmas shop. Carla watched them, a wistful look in her eye.

"I have an evening gown in my car. Heading home to finish it tonight."

I put on my coat and went outside with her. "Can I help, Carla?"

"Have you learned to sew?"

"Well, no. Is there anything useful I can do besides that? Answer the phone at the shop or greet customers?"

She eyed me, standing with the car door open. "Hmm. You could field phone calls and maybe deal with a couple of walk-ins tomorrow. I've come to rely on Irene for that in addition to her sewing skills. She's cracked a tooth, and her dentist is working her in tomorrow. You sure you don't mind, Francie?"

"I offered, right? I'd love to do something worthwhile. This visit has been awkward so far. Brad…" I stopped, reminding myself I wasn't going to make our situation worse by talking about him behind his back. Yet even Brad seemed to have something to occupy his time. I was the only one at loose ends. "Let me check with Emily. She's giving me a B&B tour tomorrow. I'll give you a ballpark time when I have it."

Carla hugged me. "Show up, and I'll tell you what to do. It'll be just like the good old days, Sis." A glint of big-sister superiority sparkled in her eye.

"Now you're scaring me," I said, laughing.

Chapter Six

BRAD AND I said goodnight to Joseph and the others and walked up the gravel drive to the lakeside cabin. Unless we were going to town, there was no need to move the car. The wind that had picked up earlier was colder now that the sun had been down a while. I shivered involuntarily, but Brad didn't notice my discomfort. Or, if he did, he chose not to put his arm around me as he used to do. That made me colder still.

Brad unlocked the cabin door and let me precede him across the threshold. The small space which should feel intimate was, instead, sad and confining. We hung up our jackets, and Brad pulled out his phone. I put the kettle on to make chamomile tea, in hopes I would sleep better tonight. His sleep had been fitful since we got here too, so I thought to offer him a cup.

"Brad, do you want a cup of chamomile tea? It helps me relax, and, in theory at least, is supposed to aid in sleep."

Several moments passed and I asked again.

"Huh?" Brad finally responded. "Francie, do you have signal here?"

"I have had. What's wrong?"

"I have zilch. Check your phone, will you?"

I pulled it out. "Well, that's weird. You're right, no service. I wonder what's up." Not caring, because I'd spoken in person this evening with everyone who mattered most to me, I plugged the phone into its charger in the living area, went back around the tiny bar, took a mug off a hook, and put a teabag into it. "What did you decide about tea?"

"Tea. Why do you keep talking about that? I have no cell service!" Brad put his jacket back on, shoved his phone into his pocket, and stalked out.

When the door slammed, the dam broke. I must have cried for half an hour. When the kettle whistled, I turned off the burner and made a cup of tea, though it was hard to drink it while sobbing. I knew this would be another night in which I would sleep very little.

I don't know how late it was when Brad came back in. I didn't hear or feel him come to bed. I had wedged myself against the slanted roof wall, and when I woke in the morning, I noticed he had done the same on the other side.

****

Emily chattered happily as she led the way from the cabin Brad and I shared. Had I done such a good job with makeup that she didn't notice the dark circles under my eyes or the sadness that enveloped me?

"So when Lillian texts to let me know which guests have arrived for breakfast, I go to that cabin to make the beds and do whatever light cleaning it needs. Most visitors tend to be neat with the cabins. I think that has to do with the small space. It's easier to deal with if you keep it neat, and people seem to inherently get that."

"Wait. What?"

"Most guests seem to—"

"No. Not that part. You said Mom *texts* you?"

"Oh, yeah. I told her it's quicker for me to be working and get a text, react to it, get back to work. The guests who are at breakfast don't know what she's doing either, or overhear her as they would if we were talking. It works well for us."

"My mother is texting." Would wonders never cease?

Emily smiled. "Lillian is awesome. I know she doesn't want me to worry about it, but I do. What she'll do when the baby comes, I mean. David and I talked again last night, and we'd both love it if I didn't have to find a babysitter in order to go back to work. We don't want somebody else being the one who watches our child learn to crawl, take her first step."

"I know what you mean, I think. I felt very fortunate Brad's income let me stay home and raise Joseph." My mind flashed back to Joseph learning to crawl and Brad being home—it must have been an evening or weekend—when Joseph took his first step. I shook my head to come back to the present. "Brad was hands-on. David will be too, I'm sure. Will he still travel all week?"

I had been lucky on that. Although Brad had always worked long days and spent part of many weekends at the office to prepare for Mondays, he'd made sure to have as much time as possible with us. When had it changed? When had Brad begun to distance himself from me—from us? I knew it was terrible that I couldn't pinpoint the time it had happened. What kind of wife and mother was I to be unaware of such a major change in our lives?

Emily unlocked a cabin and I helped her do a quick onceover. I climbed into the loft and made the bed, and she didn't protest. As her pregnancy advanced, that portion of the B&B business in particular would be difficult, if not dangerous. We were out of the cabin and on our way to the next in no time, leaving behind a sparkling clean kitchen and bathroom, dusted living area, and straightened sleeping loft. I had even washed the windows.

The weak December sun slanted through evergreens as we walked. "Living in one of these is like being inside a playhouse, but I have to admit cleaning them is a breeze," I said.

"I know, right? I had seen them on TV but didn't know how I'd do living in one. Pretty awesome."

That wasn't what I'd meant, but I didn't correct her.

By late morning, I was being instructed by Carla on how she wanted me to handle phone calls and customers who walked in. "Believe it or not, at least one person will come in here and want me to take on a new project to be finished by Christmas. You can tell them I'm not available for anything with a completion date sooner than March first. I'm swamped, even with Irene's help."

The place was mostly quiet except for the humming of Carla's sewing machine and a couple of phone calls. I wandered around the shop looking for something to straighten or dust. I ran the little electric broom, and without anything else to do, gravitated to a stack of magazines fanned out on an elegant display table. Carla's handwriting graced a professional-looking display with *Our designs in the headlines.* A list of the magazines told what page each design was on and who was wearing it. I flipped through all of them. It was great. Free publicity. No wonder Carla was buried in projects.

I set down the final magazine and arranged them as they had been before. Something caught my attention then. I examined one cover that looked familiar, though I seldom read *People*. It was three years old. Oh, weird. This was a copy of the same issue Emily had given me at her consignment store. I had stashed it away somewhere, unread. How funny to run across it here.

I put up the CLOSED sign promptly at noon and locked the door. Carla had brought her lunch, as usual, but neither of us had thought of what I would eat. I slipped out the back door and went to the rear entrance of *Chez Gwendolyn* to order takeout.

"Hey, Francie."

I was thankful for the *Chez Gwen* nametag. "Hey, Cheryl. How are you doing?"

"Great. You picking up the two specials for Brad?"

"No." My face flamed as if I'd just been

slapped. I didn't even know where Brad was. I hadn't seen him since meeting Emily this morning. Who would he be buying lunch for?

A sparkle of mischievous interest showed on her face. "Oh. Well, that's good, because if you were, I thought I had written down the time wrong. What can I help you with?"

My head whirling, I managed to order a sandwich. I carried it back to Carla's shop, knocked, and when she let me in, sat at the table in the workroom with her.

After a few minutes, Carla looked up from her hurried meal. "Aren't you going to eat your lunch, Francie? It smells great."

I shoved the Styrofoam box across the table to Carla. "Help yourself."

"What's wrong?"

"Nothing. I'm okay. Just not hungry, after all."

Chapter Seven

I WOKE UP from another night of fitful sleep, stared for a minute at the lightening skylight just a few feet above my head while I remembered where I was. With an effort, I pushed the heavy comforter away and stood up carefully in the narrow space, noting that Brad had already risen. The smell of coffee finally reached my awareness, and I pulled on my heavy robe and climbed down the ladder.

Brad was in a living room chair, head down, scowling at his phone. He looked up briefly when I alighted on the hardwood floor.

"Morning," he said in a gruff voice.

Just another day in marital Paradise. "Good morning." I poured a mug of coffee and perched on the edge of the other chair. "Bad news?"

He looked up, his brows knit. "What's that?"

"Did you get bad news?" I pointed at the smartphone.

He slid the phone into his chest pocket. "Only the worst. There's still no service."

Somebody needed to take a look at his electronics addiction. "Wow. That's horrible."

He pushed up out of the chair and stalked across the room, refilling his mug. "Thanks for the commiseration, Francie. You do realize that while we're here, this phone is my only link to making sure we still have an income. Right?"

"I realize you're constantly on that stupid phone and spend more time staring at it than talking to me. I realize *that*. Do you?"

Brad took a deep breath, his chest expanding in a way that would have made my pulse race not so long ago. His eyes closed as he composed himself for a response. "Francie, sometimes I don't know what you want from me. I'm trying to provide a livelihood for our family."

"Our family is one-third self-sufficient. Joseph

doesn't need us anymore, in case you hadn't noticed."

A corner of Brad's mouth turned up. "I'm proud of him too. Glad he's doing well in his career so soon after college. However, I might make a case that he does still need us."

"Oh really? In what way do you think he needs us?"

"I think at this point you and I are cheerleaders for our son. And friends to him."

"Do friends actually *see* each other once in a while?"

"Francie, it's too early in the day to play the baiting game. I'd love to be able to get away from work and fly out to Joseph's like you do."

He'd better not throw the *free time* Frisbee at me because I could sure throw it back. It had been our joint decision for me to stay home and be a full-time mom. I had loved every minute of it, was never bored as some of our Florida friends suggested I would be. Joseph's college years, and now his move to Colorado, had thrown me into a different time of life, and although I'd taken a few part-time jobs, nothing seemed to fit. It wasn't, however, because I didn't try to find a purpose or direction.

Brad had suggested more than once that I had *dabbled* at becoming a career-oriented person. With Joseph grown up, I'd toyed with the idea of going back to college to get another degree, since my business degree was outdated, but I had no inclination to join the ranks of those dedicated folks who commuted to a cubicle each day. I read a lot of stuff online and in business magazines that Brad subscribed to and none of it piqued my interest at all.

What degree would I get? What career would I even be interested in? I didn't know, and the whole idea of discussing these matters with anyone was intimidating. I felt like a loser. My marriage was unraveling, the closeness we once shared now turning to disdain. My career of being a full-time parent was ancient history with nothing else on the horizon. None of our friends in Florida would understand my thought process. They hadn't understood my choices up until now. I didn't want to burden Mom or the girls with my issues. They would feel bad for me, but not be able to fix it. Nobody could fix it but me. Of that I was certain, and I wasn't certain of many things these days.

Brad left, his cell phone charger in his coat pocket since the phone had run down while searching for a network. He got into the car and drove away, to where I didn't know. He had offered to take me down to Mom's or into town, but I could walk to Mom's and had no reason to go into Serendipity this morning.

Chapter Eight

ALICE AND ROBERT flew from Los Angeles to the Louisville airport, and I drove down that morning to pick them up. It wasn't a hardship; I had plenty of time, which most of the family did not. Alice's parents, Tassia and Jack Campbell, were doing some kind of project to their house. It seemed to be a *thing* around Serendipity this year to have the house partly torn up right at the holidays. So they were glad to let me do the drive to the city and back.

Brad surprised me by not minding that I took the car. At his request, I dropped him off in town on the way.

"What will you do downtown?" I asked, as we entered the city limits.

"You always tell me I'm missing the charm of

Serendipity. That I should give it a chance."

"Ah." That told me nothing.

I couldn't remember an instance of him spending an entire morning in downtown Serendipity on his own, but I didn't want to examine the possibilities too closely. I reassured myself that at least he wasn't meeting a woman in a discreet location. In all of Serendipity, there *was* no discreet location. The gossip tree had branches and roots everywhere. Brad couldn't have found another woman here, of all places. I knew it was ridiculous, yet my brain kept trying to convince me of the possibility.

After leaving him at the same corner where he had dropped me the other day, I headed south on State Road 135. I tried to calm my mind with innocent ways Brad could spend his morning. Mani-Pedi at the nail place? There was a drastic unlikelihood that made me smile. He could stop in and visit Jennifer Kincaid at *Emily's Dreams*, or pop into the antiques store. Chat with Carla at *Creations* or Jim in his law office. But he wouldn't stop in to see my siblings—had never been close to any of them, and if he wanted to talk to Jim, he could do that at the farm this evening.

No, Brad was more likely to hover over a series of cups of coffee and pastries at *Something Sweet*, where he could use their free Wi-Fi. He had his laptop bag with him after all. And his beloved phone.

Instead of using the cell phone lot, I parked and waited inside the airport. I always love to people-watch, and airports are a great place to do that. Observing the tearful hellos and goodbyes, I was reminded of *Love, Actually*—one of my favorite movies. I'd seen it so many times, I could almost recite the script from memory. I stood there reliving my favorite story lines and trying to block the flashes of scene in which the character played by Alan Rickman is sucked into a relationship with his *very* friendly secretary.

Brad's secretary wasn't like that. I knew her somewhat, and sure, she was loyal to him and willing to work extra if he needed her to do so. She was pretty, and younger than I, and unattached... But Brad wouldn't do that to me.

Would he?

A young family of four walked past, pulling

wheeled carry-on bags. A magazine hit the floor, but no one seemed to notice. I picked it up, and by hurrying, caught up with them.

I tapped the woman on the shoulder. "Excuse me, but you dropped this."

She stopped and turned, looked at the magazine and then smiled at me. "Oh, sorry—didn't realize I was littering. I've finished that, so if you want to read it, help yourself. Or just recycle." She turned away and the group moved toward the escalator to baggage claim.

I recognized the magazine cover. It was another copy of *People*—just like the one Emily had given me, which was also in Carla's shop. My palms started to sweat at the strange coincidence.

When I looked up, Alice and Robert had stopped right in front of me. Alice laughed, hugging me.

"Earth to Francie. What was going through that busy brain of yours, girlfriend?"

I gave myself a mental shake and came back to the moment. "Sorry. 'Tis the season, I suppose. So many things going on." I held out the magazine.

"Somebody gave me this. The strange thing is Carla has a copy of the same issue at her shop…" My sentence trailed off, since I knew the oddity of the magazine might not seem unusual to anyone but me.

They were both smiling, glad to see me, and not caring about my little coincidence. I tossed the magazine into a nearby recycle bin. It was creepy for the darn thing to show up again, but that didn't mean I had to read it. At this point, part of me was afraid to look too closely at its contents.

Robert shook my hand. "So nice of you to pick us up, Francie. Alice still doesn't trust me to drive in Indiana, even though I'm allowed behind the wheel anywhere else."

I shook a finger at her. "Now, Alice, you know Robert could probably do just fine as long as he avoids trying to drive around Serendipity's town square. I'd put that up against any driving hazard in the world."

Laughing at my joke, which wouldn't be all that funny for drivers who enter the square without forewarning, we went down the escalator to luggage claim. I put an arm around Alice's shoulders as Robert rushed to the carousel, having spotted their two bags. "You look happy. Robert's a lucky guy."

"The luck, if you want to call it that, is on both sides. And you're right, we're super happy." She looked into my eyes. "What about you, Francie? I'm worried about you. We all are."

"Oh, nothing to worry about. Mostly because worry won't help. Brad and I—we'll figure it out." If only that was true. So far we hadn't made much progress toward working out problems. We'd spent plenty of time blaming each other and reopening old wounds. If our problem had started with, or had led to, him having an affair, what then? Would he put an end to the situation and ask for my forgiveness? If he asked, could I get past the pain and betrayal and forgive him?

Could our marriage survive, or were we near the end of it? And if we were near the end, what happened next? Would Joseph cope okay or feel cheated to lose the solid underpinning of parents who were married to each other? How long had it been since that solid underpinning had been a *happy* marriage?

"Hello?" Alice was in front of me, had both

hands on my shoulders. I saw Robert approach with the bags. "It's clear that a girlfriend night is a first priority."

"Good luck with that. Everybody's busy."

She rolled her eyes. "Carla is a slave to that shop these days. Mel can surely spend some time away from work. Does anybody buy real estate at Christmas? Don't worry, we'll get together. I'm not too proud to play the Guilt Card. You and I traveled all this way for a big, happy holiday, and I'm determined for us to have one." She smiled at Robert. "Right, honey?"

I turned toward the parking garage, and in my peripheral vision saw Robert lean down and kiss Alice's cheek. "Whatever you say, boss. We all know I can barely function in this atmosphere, so you're leading and I'm following."

"Robert is talented with the Guilt Card," Alice said. "This year it's Christmas in Serendipity, and next year we'll spend it with his family in the St. Louis area. I can't tell you how many times I've heard about the family traditions he's missing with his parents and siblings. Doesn't matter that we spent a week there last month."

Robert made a grumbling sound. "Thanksgiving is *not* Christmas."

Alice giggled, putting an arm through his. "You heard it here first, folks. Francie, we had Christmas with Robert's kids a couple of days ago at our house. I'm not getting any points for that, of course."

Robert winked at me when Alice wasn't looking. It was always fun to be with them. An outsider might take their bickering seriously, but I knew it was the way they always interacted with each other. It was funny and beautiful. I tried not to let it be yet another heartbreaking reminder of the state of my relationship with Brad.

The drive back to Serendipity was more fun than the solo drive to Louisville and was over too soon. I hugged Alice and Robert and her mom when I left them in the kitchen of the house where Alice had grown up. Alice followed me to the car, stood by it as I slid behind the wheel. "We'll have a girlfriend night, Francie. You can depend on it."

I knew she could make it happen, that with her prompting, Carla would find a way to set aside the time.

And I knew Alice would make the plea all about me. As much as I had avoided the questions of concern, I was wearing down. If Mel, Carla, and Alice wanted to do an intervention, I wasn't sure I could resist, or that I even wanted to.

Chapter Nine

A COUPLE OF days later, Emily had a doctor's appointment, and I volunteered to clean the cabins for her. When a guest arrived for breakfast at the house, Mom texted me. It was still a shocker to see a message like *Cabin3 Brkfst* coming into my phone from her. Tidying the tiny space was quick work but gave me more of a sense of purpose than I'd had in a long time. Maybe when I got home, I could find a service job of some sort.

I finished quickly and took a few minutes to sparkle up the cabin Brad and I were staying in. Then I went into Mom's house through the back door so I wouldn't interrupt if she still had guests in the dining room. Daisy rose when I stepped into the kitchen from the mud room. Her tail thumped expectantly, and I knelt on the floor, talking to her and petting her.

Apparently, she wasn't allowed in the dining room with the B&B folks, but it suited me fine to have this time to spoil her. Daisy edged closer so we weren't separated at all. She was warm, thrilled to see me, and expected nothing but my undivided attention. I almost remembered when Brad was like that.

I heard Mom saying goodbye on the other side of the door to the dining room and the front door closed. A couple of minutes later, she came into the kitchen carrying a tray with her silver coffee service on it.

"Oh, Francie. What a nice surprise."

I helped clear the dining table, fill the dishwasher, and hand-wash and dry the items Mom never trusted to technology. I made half a pot of coffee, and the three of us relaxed in the cozy kitchen. Daisy was poised halfway between Mom and me, ever watchful in case a bit of food might present itself. Mom gestured, and the devoted dog put her head in Mom's lap and sighed.

Mom's smile was tired as she stroked Daisy's

sleek head. "Thank you for your help this morning. Your timing is perfect. I've been wanting to talk to you alone."

She took a deep breath, looking down at Daisy for a long moment before meeting my eyes again. My stomach lurched at the look in her eyes. Something big was up with Mom, and I didn't feel ready to deal with whatever it was.

"Francie, I haven't said this to any of the others, but I'm thinking of slowing down. The Christmas tree farm was always more your father's dream than mine. When he was alive and we worked together, it didn't seem like so much effort. Harry loved every minute he spent with those trees and his customers."

I sank into my chair a little, briefly relieved that the discussion wasn't going to be about Brad and me. But my mind was racing. What was Mom saying? Was she sick? She looked the same as always, though perhaps not quite as energetic. I chose my words carefully, trying not to sound as worried as I was. "I know. I never expected to like Christmas anymore after Dad died."

She nodded. "Neither did I. As time passes, the hurt changes." She looked into my eyes. "It doesn't go away, but it's easier to deal with. Do you find that to be true, Francie?"

"Yes. That's a good way to describe it. When I walk out on the farm, there are still times I expect Dad to come out from behind a big tree with that wide grin of his and tell me what's new this year or what he planned to do next year to make the season even better for the customers." I didn't know how Mom handled Dad's loss so well. Or—maybe she wasn't handling it as well as I thought.

"So, you're thinking of slowing down. That makes sense. With the B&B year-round—"

"It isn't just the bed and breakfast. I'm tired, honey. I need a break, and to be honest, I think I deserve one."

"Oh. A break." When had Mom taken any kind of vacation? She and Dad had always seemed content to be at home with us kids coming to visit whenever. They had made the trip to see Brad, Joseph, and me in Florida a few times, but Dad especially seemed to feel out of place when they did. "A break is probably a great idea, Mom. Are you going to take a—a trip?" I couldn't imagine it. My mom getting in her car to drive somewhere in order to amuse herself. Or wilder still, my mom getting onto a plane for an actual vacation. The images just wouldn't appear.

She laughed. "Don't look so stricken, Francie. People my age do travel, you know. I'm not ancient. I want to learn new things and see more of the world."

"I'm sorry. I didn't mean to suggest you're—you know—*past* it." But I guess I had assumed she was. "So, you are going to travel. That's awesome, Mom. It really is. On your own?" I heard my voice squeak on the last word caused by the spike in my stress level.

She shrugged. "I've looked into some different options. And another thing is that I need to downsize. Francie, do you remember what Emily went through after her car accident?"

Emily had a wreck when I was staying with Mom a few months after Dad died. But I had gone home with Brad and Joseph after Christmas when Emily was in a rehab facility. At some point when she got home again, she opened the consignment shop on the square and had caused quite a stir by slipping extra items into customers' bags—items that, sooner or later, made quite an impact on those customers' lives. She had given me the outdated copy of *People* magazine when I stopped into the shop with Carla during a visit back home. One of these days maybe I would read it to see what Emily thought was special in it for me.

I really had no concept of what Emily had gone through, just remembered snippets. "I'm sketchy on details," I said.

Mom wrapped her hands around the steaming cup of coffee. "The short version is that Emily chose to change her life. The wreck got her attention, I suppose, and she decided she couldn't move into her future without offloading things—including many of her possessions."

"Oh, right. When she opened the store, it was her own stuff she was selling and giving away." I paused, watching Mom's face. "And you liken this to losing Dad and needing to move into your own future by…umm…*offloading*?"

She took a sip, smiling at me over her cup. "I need to downsize. I *don't* need this big house, don't need to spend time taking care of it. If not for Joseph's enthusiasm, I wouldn't have started working on the upstairs rooms."

I could have done without that particular result of Joseph's enthusiasm. Brad and I would have been rather comfortably sharing that large room with its two single beds. But—*wait a minute.* Was Mom thinking of selling the house?

She took my hand, searched my face. "Don't overthink it, honey. I just needed to tell you while you're here. Not sure when I'll bring it up with the others. Of course, I've been through all of it with your father. Rather a one-sided conversation, but still. Your father and I never had secrets from each other beyond Christmas or birthday gifts. We shared everything, big or small, all those years..."

My mind was whirling with images. Mom jetting off to places unknown (to me), finding a new life that became more important to her than the farm or her family. Future Christmases without not only Dad but also Mom, either because she was off seeing the world or because she had died.

Was illness the real reason for her decision to slow down? Maybe she was sick, and instead of a sudden death like Dad's, hers would be lengthy and painful. And she was preparing the rest of us by handing over the reins of the farm and separating herself from us by traveling, so that we became accustomed to her absence.

Also in the whirl of images was the corner of the tree farm that she and Dad had given me, currently sporting a nice crop of evergreens. But would it become the impressive entryway to a new housing development when the farm ceased to exist? I could imagine the headquarters of, for instance, *Evergreen Springs Home Owners Association* sitting on the spot that could have held my home. The existing houses—Mom's, Jim and Melissa's, David and Emily's, and Carla's—would be torn down, along with the outbuildings, Christmas shop, and the tiny cabins, since they wouldn't fit in with the massive new builds with postage stamp yards. All the trees would be ripped out too and burned. Once the clubhouse was completed, the entryway would be landscaped with slow-growth evergreens that would never grace anyone's living room or even have their scent appreciated by a passerby, since no one would be on foot—they would always drive past it in their gleaming SUVs.

A noise pulled me out of the nightmarish reverie.

Mom shook her head at me, a crooked smile on her face. "Your phone, honey."

The caller ID told me it was Brad. I turned the phone face down, and the noise stopped. He could leave a message. I was not in the mood for more bad news. How sad, because back in the day I would have poured out my heart to him, but now I knew he didn't want it.

Not the bad news. And not my heart.

****

I was on the edge of tears for the rest of the day. Mom hadn't shared any specifics with me, beyond the fact that she wanted to downsize "sooner, rather than later." Good-bye to any last hopes for a festive family

Christmas. Instead of the holiday being *merry and bright*, everything was wrong.

With Mom slowing down, all responsibilities of the farm would fall to Jim, who had a busy law practice, a wife, and son.

Carla was too caught up in work to spend time with us girls.

Emily was likely—for a good reason of course—to ditch her job with the B&B.

Jim seemed colder than usual to Brad, and vice versa.

Joseph was trying to play elf for everyone. That part made me sadder than anything, because I loved his enthusiasm and optimism, even though I expected them both to be crushed by The Real World before long.

Chapter Ten

SOMEHOW ALICE MANAGED to pry Carla out of her shop for the evening. Instead of going out of town, as in Louisville, or even the limited possibilities of going out *on* the town of Serendipity, we congregated at Mel and Jim's cabin on the northwest corner of the farm.

Carla looked happy to be with us for a few hours of kicking back. When Mel opened a bottle of wine and started pouring, Carla made the first toast.

"I'd like to drink to the fabulous Irene Glass, who is saving my sanity since I hired her. Also to Alice's mom for filling in at the Christmas shop so Mel and Francie can have the night off. Seriously, ladies, even though we're grown-ups, where would we be without our mothers and surrogate mothers?"

Goosebumps popped up on my arms. Where

indeed would we be—and how soon were Carla and I going to find out?

"What's wrong, Francie?" Mel pinned me with a stare.

"Nothing. I just had a chill." I moved to a chair nearer the crackling fire that burned in the fireplace built of stones Jim had found on the farm. When the land was sold, no one would appreciate what a labor of love and loss the creation of this home had been for Jim after his disastrous first marriage and before he and Mel rediscovered each other.

I took a less-than-delicate sip of wine and reminded myself that Mom didn't want me to tell anyone about our conversation. I didn't want to carry this awful secret alone, yet I couldn't break her confidence.

Carla pulled a chair up next to mine. "You going to finally tell us what's going on with you and Brad?" she whispered.

Alice and Mel were in the kitchen assembling a buffet for our dinner. I didn't have workable cooking facilities in the tiny cabin and nobody wanted Carla to cook—ever—so my contribution had been a couple bags of Mom's cookies purchased from the Christmas shop. Carla had picked up some salads and fruit at the grocery. It didn't matter what the spread turned out to be, since the conversation had already caused me to lose my appetite.

"Carla, let's just keep things light, okay?"

"No, it's not okay. The four of us support each other, Francie. You've always been great to help out any of us who need it. Now it's your turn to be on the receiving end of the support, and it's high time you *let us help you.*"

Alice and Mel walked into the room just as Carla's last words were hanging in the air, having been spoken a little loudly. They looked at us, then at each other, and without saying anything, set out the food. Mel turned on some music—Christmas music, of course. Is there any other kind in December? And, if so, who cares?

We sang along with *Jingle Bells*, but when Bing Crosby started into *I'll Be Home for Christmas*, we fell silent. Everyone was near tears.

"I never hear this without thinking of Dad," Carla whispered, and we all nodded. Many people—those who knew him well or only slightly as the guy who ran the Christmas tree farm, said Harry Standish had been as near to Santa Claus as anybody. *I'll Be Home for Christmas* had been his favorite holiday song, and he had whistled it until the whole family thought we'd go nuts from the sound. Now we'd all love to hear his rendition one more time. But it was too late. Too late for a lot of things.

"Nothing lasts forever."

The girls looked at me. I hadn't realize I'd spoken the words aloud.

Mel topped off my drink. "You have something to tell us, Francie? We're here for you."

All they had on their minds was to help me figure out what to do about my relationship with Brad. Since my conversation with Mom, the furor in my head had changed. And now I realized I needed to talk to Brad. There was a lot I had to say to him. I hoped it wasn't too late for that too.

"I know you're trying to be supportive, girls.

You have no idea what comfort and courage that gives me." Their three faces, so dear to me, spoke volumes without saying more. I was carried in their thoughts and on their prayers. So was Brad, no doubt. Which was as it should be.

But many things were *not* as they should be. Unlike any other time, I looked forward to the end of our girls' night. For once, the important conversations I would have today would not take place in the presence of these women who were my dearest friends.

Two or three hours later, having switched from wine to cocoa, and said good night to the girls, I was ready to start the second earth-shaking discussion of the day.

Chapter Eleven

BEFORE LEAVING MEL'S house, I asked to "borrow" a bottle of wine. I let myself into the cabin. Brad was hunched over his laptop, looking uncomfortable in one of the small chairs. For a moment, I was transported to the early days of our marriage when I worked whatever part-time job I could find and Brad was in law school, studying incessantly. Back then I would walk behind him and massage his shoulders, and he'd lean back and look up at me. I'd kiss him, and sometimes the studying waited until later. Like I said, we were newlyweds at the time.

Brad raised his head and met my eyes. "Hi, Francie."

I held up the bottle. "Hi. I come bringing gifts. Actually, I almost stole it from Mel. She opened it, since I was sure there's no appropriate tool in the teensy kitchen." I demonstrated the looseness of the cork. "Care for a glass?"

His brows rose. "Sure."

A couple minutes later I was back, having poured wine into two *Standish Christmas Tree Farm B&B* coffee mugs. I handed one to him and sat in the other chair. "A little shy on stemware here."

He smiled and sipped. "Hmm. Not bad." He shut the laptop lid and set it on the floor beside him. "You ladies have fun?"

I shrugged, wondering how long we could keep up a pleasant conversation. "I guess. I mean, sure, it's always good to get together. It'd be nice if we could manage an evening that's not in the busiest time of the year, but I'll take this over nothing." I pointed at the laptop. "So, you have Wi-Fi?"

Brad watched me, waiting. "Downloaded some reading earlier. Okay, Francie. What you really want to talk about is..."

He'd known me so long and knew me better than anyone—better even than Mom or my best girlfriends, didn't he?

I took a deep breath. "Brad, I'm worried about Mom. She—she said some things to me today and asked me not to tell anyone else. But it's more than I can carry alone. She said she and Dad never had secrets, so I'm hoping she won't mind that I talk to you." How could I expect him to be willing to listen to my problems when we'd been communicating so poorly? But I'd let the words out. I *didn't* want to carry this alone. "Maybe if I say this out loud, it won't be so scary to me. You're pragmatic. You can help me see it clearly." I swallowed. "If you don't mind."

He tipped his head to one side. "You have my undivided attention."

Boy, was I glad for the lack of Internet service. Even without it, though, Brad could have chosen not to hear what was on my mind, and I couldn't have blamed him. Instead, he listened silently, nodding or asking a clarifying question when needed. When I finished telling him what Mom had laid on me, I felt lighter.

He was quiet for several minutes. I refilled his wine mug.

"Francie, I appreciate you confiding in me. Do you see signs of Lillian being unwell? She seems the same to me. Just tired, but the whole family is tired this time of year."

"I haven't noticed anything unusual. None of the others has mentioned any concern."

He nodded. "It's her life, after all. She's worked hard for many years, and if she's ready to downsize and do some traveling, we should support her in that decision."

That made sense, and I knew I should feel the same way. Still, he wasn't as involved as my siblings and I were. It wouldn't break his heart to see the farm sold and whatever came next. But I didn't say those things, wanting to avoid additional confrontation if I could.

"I get what you're saying, and I agree. I want Mom to take a break, see the world, whatever she wants. She deserves to have a life of her own choosing." I stopped, not wanting to sound—or even worse, to be—selfish. "I'd hate for us to lose the farm though. But I don't know how we could continue without Mom overseeing so much. She and Jim hold it together."

Brad walked over and poured himself more wine. He held up the bottle indicating I could have a refill too, but I shook my head.

I felt a little better having discussed my concerns with Brad. But why wasn't he more concerned about the situation? If not for himself, or for me, surely he could see how losing the farm could impact Joseph.

****

That night, I lay awake a long time reading. That same daggone magazine I had seen at Carla's shop, and recycled at the airport, had been on the top of a tall stack in a cardboard carton Mel was going to donate to the Friends of the Library bookstore. Exasperated at seeing it again, I asked if she cared whether I took it. When she shook her head *no,* I stuck it in my handbag.

I read the issue from cover to cover. I'd just finished when I heard Brad shut down his laptop and plug it in to recharge, then go to the bathroom in preparation for coming to bed. I shut off the reading lamp and pretended to be asleep. I doubt I fooled Brad, but he didn't say anything. He didn't whisper my name or reach for me. I wondered if he noticed I wasn't at the very edge of the mattress tonight.

Chapter Twelve

THE NEXT MORNING once Brad had left, I picked up the magazine again. I quickly flipped past the items that had been highlighted in Carla's copy. In it, sticky notes marked the pages on which gowns by *Creations* had graced a Paris gala and the Academy Awards. The article I wanted to reread, the one that had me in tears last night, was written by a recent widow. She was blaming herself for not seeing the signs that led up to her actor husband's massive heart attack. A relatively fit man in his late forties, he had literally worked himself to death. She was left with a palatial home, pool, landscaped lawns, and the money to pay all the personnel who took care of it. And she was left with overwhelming regret.

The final paragraph seemed to jump off the page

at me, as it had done last night: *If I could trade all these things in exchange for my husband's life, I would do it without hesitation. Our marriage was so much happier before we started the rat race for money, fame, and all these beautiful belongings. We sometimes laughed that our best days together were in our first apartment, when life was simple. I didn't need more than that. I wish I had told him so.*

Dad had a massive heart attack and was gone. But at least he had loved his work. Brad was working inhuman hours at a job that seemed to be eating him alive. He needed to make a change, and I needed to help him see that fact.

Greeting customers in the Christmas shop that night lifted my spirits, as usual. Tonight I was working with Mom and Mel. Matthew was spending the evening with Jared's son, Miles, his best friend. Like everyone else in the family, I was looking forward to knowing when Carla and Jared would get married. After all Carla's years of designing beautiful clothes, including some stunning wedding gowns, I wanted to see what she would choose for her own wedding.

Perhaps it was selfish of me to want to be present for that uplifting experience. And I realized I didn't want to just fly or drive here to see her wedding either. I wanted to *live* here. Was there a way I could build my house on the corner after all these years and take over Mom's part of the work? Was there any way Brad would agree to the move? If not, would I do it without him?

No, I realized, I would not. We had troubles, but our marriage was important to me. The commitment we had made more than two decades ago was worth honoring. And, rough times notwithstanding, I loved Brad. The fact that he had taken the time to listen to my concerns about Mom and the farm gave me some hope that he still cared for me.

Could this marriage be saved? Absolutely, but we both had to want to save it.

I paid more attention than usual to what Mom did in the Christmas shop. She was pleasant and fun with each customer, going out of her way to be sure everyone received good treatment. Unlike many stores I'd been in, shoppers didn't seem to mind waiting a few minutes for their turn and were rewarded for their patience. Free cocoa and wassail were popular but didn't seem to be required. Sometimes customers bought a packet of a mix, but often they just said *Thank you*, paid for the rest of their purchases, and left in a blast of cold air, saying *Merry Christmas!* as they closed the door. It didn't matter though. No amount of frigid temperatures could touch the basic warmth of the shop—the kind created not from cranking up the furnace but by smiling and caring about each person who came through.

I straightened a display of blown glass ornaments. Mel was nearby, putting out the last of the foot-tall, hand-knit "Gingerbread men" being sold on consignment by some ladies in the local nursing home.

"Joseph has a theory about the farm providing some kind of touchstone for people during the holidays—especially this year. Something about a connection with a positive history and reminder of old-fashioned family time and values, and so on," I said.

Mel finished her task and turned to me. "Interesting. He may well be right. What a year we've all been through. I imagine most of us are more ready than usual for a happy new year. Wow, if we are providing a bit of hope to folks, that sure puts straightening shelves and making wassail in a different light."

"Yes. Doesn't it?"

She moved away to another part of the shop and I took a look around, seeing the place in a new way. What if the Standish tree farm shut down? It would not only be a huge loss to our family but also to the community. To the ladies who knitted those gingerbread men and created other handmade items, enjoying the tasks and the extra money. To the local young people who helped Jim at the farm during off-season months. And who knew who else would be impacted by closing the farm?

It wasn't just a selfish hope of mine that the farm could continue. No, it was bigger than that. And because it was, I knew the time had come to bare my soul to Brad. The worst that could happen was that he'd divorce me, and the best was he would see things my way. Now and looking toward the future.

Mom told me I have a propensity to overthink, and maybe that's what I'd been doing about Brad and me for a long time. Thinking, fearing, lashing out. What I needed to do was something much different. A lot was riding on what I would do and say. It might very well be the most important discussion Brad and I ever had.

Chapter Thirteen

IT WAS CHRISTMAS Eve. We'd shut down the tree lot and the Christmas shop around eight.

"I'll see everyone for lunch at noon," Mom reminded us as we separated. I'd taken some time in her kitchen to prepare a couple of pies for the family pitch-in.

Joseph gave me and Brad each a hug. "Night, you two. I'm in charge of the ham and the turkey and dressing. Gotta study to make sure I'm ready to take on this mantle."

We laughed with him.

"Good night, son," Brad said, clapping him on the shoulder before Joseph trotted to catch up with Mom.

I looked up at Brad's proud face. "It's great to

see him so happy," I said. "Part of it is making others happy. Do you notice that? He's got that Santa thing going on, kind of like Dad." Joseph didn't look like Harry Standish at all. He looked like Brad had at his age.

Brad nodded and adjusted the scarf around his neck. His thin Florida blood had thickened a little in our time here but still had a ways to go to be comfortable in forty degrees with a stiff wind blowing. "I still can't believe the way that room is decorated. The one he's staying in. I can see it being Joseph's room any time he wants to visit here. Who else could fall asleep with Rudolph staring down from the ceiling? I don't suppose the upstairs of Lillian's house will really become part of the B&B, do you?"

I hesitated. "I imagine you're right on both counts. Funny how things work out. Uh, what time is it?" Time to stall, say anything instead of bringing up the topic we needed to discuss.

Brad shrugged. I heard, rather than saw it, with the *swish* of his nylon ski jacket. "Don't know the time. I left my phone in the cabin."

"Wow. Really?"

"Yep. Who's going to call me on Christmas Eve? Certainly not the office."

Not even your secretary? I might have asked a few days ago.

"And if they did, I wouldn't answer. I'm starting to like having no cell service in the cabin. It's like a mini vacation every time I step in there."

"That's a big deal. I mean, you've been on that phone or laptop so much during this trip."

"I'm sorry. I know it's been rude of me, Francie. As Joseph said, I would have punished him for behaving that way at the table or when someone else was around wanting to talk." He reached down, took my mittened hand in his leather glove. "My only defense is that I've been working on something for both of us."

"What—what's that?"

"Something that is finally coming together, to make our future a happier one."

"Oh. You made partner?" The goal he had worked for. It would ruin everything.

He laughed, the unexpected sound wrapping me in warmth, then softening in the surrounding pine trees.

"Nope. Something much better." He stopped me with a tug on my hand, and looked down into my eyes. My heartrate quickened. The gathering darkness made the moment more sensual. "I've found a way for you to have what you've always wanted, Francie."

My heart sank. What now? A bigger house? A pool with *Blind Justice* emblazoned in the floor in mosaic tile? More impressive cars for both of us? None of which he'd be able to enjoy very much, since he was working all the time to pay for them. And none of which I cared about. All I wanted—all I had ever wanted—was to love, and be loved, and to do something worthwhile with my time.

Chapter Fourteen

WHEN BRAD EXPLAINED what he'd been up to, I couldn't believe what he was telling me.

"You're going into business with my *brother*, and kept it from me?"

"I didn't want to talk about it too soon, in case Jim and I weren't able to come to terms on everything. He and I agreed to keep it to ourselves."

I crossed my arms over my chest. "Is that right?"

"Yes, it is. I know how much you love being in Serendipity with your family and your history here. You may not realize I do listen to what you say, and notice how sad you are when we leave here each time. The strange thing is that the town, and the tree farm, have become important to me too. I never expected that. To be honest, I tried for years *not* to get sucked into the whole small town mentality. But after witnessing the magic that Christmas Eve when Melissa and Matthew had just returned, and being part of Jim and Melissa's Christmas wedding..." He rubbed a hand over his face. "Well, it finally hit me."

"What hit you?"

"That you belong here. But more than that, so do I. Something happens to me when I'm in Serendipity. I'm a better person. More relaxed. Kinder. I tried hard to take those feelings back to Florida, but they dissipated like snowflakes on a July beach. Only thing I could figure out was to create a way for us to move here. Lucky for me the partnership didn't come through. If it had, I'd have struggled to make the right decision and turn it down."

"But you've been working toward that partnership forever, Brad."

"I know. And now I look back on the years of sixty-plus hour work weeks, handling cases I would never have taken if the choice had been mine, it's hard not to feel I wasted my entire life."

"Yet when I asked you to cut back and spend more time at home—"

"I didn't have a choice, Francie. You know that."

"So you said, many times." But he could have chosen years ago to take another look at his life, couldn't he? If he had done that, so many things might have been different.

Brad tipped his head, watching me. "I hope you aren't trying to imagine what our lives might have looked like if I'd offered to pick up and move to your hometown years ago. That's a waste of time and a sure way to unhappiness."

"What do you expect me to do then? Congratulate you for staying at a job that sucked out your soul?"

"You were happy enough to spend the money that soul-sucking job generated. Remember that."

"I *had* to spend money, Brad. We were expected to maintain a lifestyle appropriate for a partner in the firm, in anticipation of it happening. The expensive home with a pool and lawn service, membership in the right organizations, appearances at the right events."

"Are you going to tell me you hated all that, Francie? As I recall, you seemed to enjoy it."

I took a deep breath and expelled it. I needed to let go of the anger and frustration that had built inside of me over the last few years. It had done nothing but poison our relationship.

"I did enjoy it, at first. For several years, in fact. But as Joseph got older and I was the only one who had time to attend most of his school athletic events, the money your job brought in wasn't worth the lost...memories." I had almost said *the lost closeness*, but was hesitant to do so. The ice between us seemed to be breaking, but I was afraid to move too fast.

He put his hands on my shoulders. "This is an opportunity to start over, Francie. Are you interested in doing that? Are you willing to give our marriage another chance? The price our house will bring on the Florida real estate market will easily build whatever you want on your corner of the tree farm, with plenty left over as a cushion."

My shoulders sagged as more stress drained

from my body. "There's nothing I want more in this world than to fix our marriage, Brad. I'm so sorry I couldn't see a way to do it before. I've felt hopeless, and it turned into bitterness." What a thing to admit, and I didn't even realize it before the words came out of my mouth.

He crushed me to him. It was hard to breathe, but I didn't care. I clung to Brad as if he were about to be ripped away from me. For a time it had seemed that was happening, but we were giving each other a second chance.

I spoke in a low voice, "But I don't...I don't really want to build a house. I think we could be happy in Mom's house."

Brad pulled back, wearing a crooked grin. "Live with your mother? I don't know about that. I love Lillian—don't get me wrong—but to live with her full-time seems like risking a perfectly cordial relationship."

"Not live with her. Mom is serious about downsizing. I can't get her to say just what she has in mind. Maybe a smaller home built on the corner, or perhaps she wants to live in an RV and do some traveling. I think she may make an announcement to the whole family when we're together for Christmas lunch. Mom is realizing she doesn't have to continue to hold the farm together. If the family wants to keep it going, we'll find a way to make that happen."

I took a deep breath. "I'm interested in taking it over, Brad. I want to run the tree farm."

"You—*what*?"

I nodded, entertained by the surprise on his face. "All our married life I've taken care of you and Joseph, been the support behind the success. That was great because I enjoyed doing it. But once Joseph was out on his own and you were pushing me away—" I held up a hand to stop his protest. "You kept so much bottled up inside, Brad. Now I'm beginning to understand what some of it was. And my reaction was half the problem." I shook my head, regretting what we had put each other through. "Anyway, I want to run the tree farm, work outside, do the financials, the whole thing."

Just saying it made me scared about the amount of work I was talking about. "I'll figure out a way to keep the Christmas shop and B&B cabins. Emily can decide about her own work with the B&B, and I'll fill in with local people who need jobs. There are plenty of good folks in Serendipity who could use the work. I'm excited about the possibilities."

Brad smiled. "I guess if I had paid more attention, I might have realized what you were thinking after your mom's conversation about slowing down. But I've been haunting Jim's office during his time between clients, plying him with carryout from *Chez Gwen*. The rest of the time, I've been studying Indiana law on my laptop and phone like my life depends on it. Because I think it does." He let out a long, relieved breath. "It's beautiful how this is all working out. I didn't expect everything to fall into place quite so neatly." He chuckled. "Almost in spite of our planning."

"You'll have to get used to that sort of thing if we're going to live in Serendipity permanently."

He gently pulled me close, and kissed me. "So true. As long as you're by my side, Francie, I can get used to anything."

Chapter Fifteen

WE STEPPED INTO the tiny cabin, which felt cozy now instead of confining. It all seemed to be perfect, or in the process of becoming that way. Only one thing was missing—one thing I'd been thinking about a lot, ever since Melissa and Jim were reunited through a set of circumstances that were so farfetched I wouldn't have believed it, if I hadn't witnessed it with my own eyes. Emily and David, Alice and Robert, Carla and Jared. After all these years of marriage, was it too much to wish Brad and I had been brought together by a touch of magic?

I said as much to my husband, touching his face and kissing his lips gently, to reassure him I was more than fine with our non-magical start.

He kissed me, long and slow. "Francie, is your

memory going? I mean, you do remember how we met, right?"

"School. Lots of couples meet in college, Brad. That's not unusual."

"Think harder. The classroom where we met— that first day of my junior year, when you were a sweet, innocent freshman. I can still picture it. Small classroom with no desks, just a handful of chairs. We talked for an hour or more, not realizing it had been that long. And it turned out we were the only people who had the wrong room on our schedule. Remember when we checked with the office?"

I could see it now too. My first day of classes on the big, beautiful, and intimidating, IU-Bloomington campus. "Right. I was super nervous. You were older, and so handsome. I kept expecting more students to come in, and the professor, and when they didn't, it was like a gift. Otherwise, I would have clammed up. And that next day, after we got to the right classroom, we had coffee afterward."

"And from that day to this one, I've never wanted any other woman, Francie. *Ever*. For me, at least, it was love at first sight. We can call it magic, or a pleasant coincidence."

"I guess when you look back, it's easier to see the magic moments," I said.

Brad's eyes crinkled in amusement and part of me melted to be the object again of his special looks and complete focus. But now I thought about it, perhaps he hadn't stopped looking at me that way. Maybe I'd been more consumed about what was wrong with our relationship, and wasn't recognizing what was right. What had always been right.

Like the simple fact that we loved each other and belonged together.

He pulled me even closer, and his kisses sent shivers all over my body. It had been too long since we'd really been together. What a waste of time—but we wouldn't make that mistake again. Neither of us would allow it.

"Let's expect more in our future," Brad said. "More magic moments of all sorts."

****

A few hours later I woke up in the arms of the man I had loved for so long. Instead of being annoyed by his snoring, I felt fortunate he was holding me, breathing regularly, and that when I lay my head on his chest, his heart beat strong. Contented, I looked up at the stars sparkling beyond the skylight. I thought it incredible that, all these years, Brad and I had had that bit of magic and I hadn't recognized it.

I believe there must be a reason our story played out the way it did. The time away from Serendipity hadn't been wasted. We had learned and grown, raised our son, been part of a community. Connections Joseph made at Florida State resulted in the job he now has and loves.

Joseph's contribution to our happily-ever-after became apparent the next morning when Brad and I walked into Mom's house hand in hand. Joseph's face lit up when he saw us, and he admitted he had encouraged Mom to tear up the extra bedrooms so Brad and I were thrown together in the cabin. Our tech-smart son had also rigged the cabin to be a reflector for any type of cell signal. In effect, it became a mini *parent trap*.

With his parents straightened out, I hoped that Joseph would be open to finding his own life partner. Maybe he'd meet her in Colorado. After all, serendipity—happy surprises—aren't limited to the little town in Indiana where I grew up.

I could visualize the way our lives might look when we moved into Mom's house and she was doing her own thing. Even a short time ago, all of these possibilities were unimagined, or scary—at least, to me.

This Christmas season was full of surprises. What a blessing that the road not taken turned out to be the one that led us home.

The End

...or is it The Beginning?

A Note From the Author

Thank you so very much for reading Francie and Brad's story! When I first planned this book, it was going to be very different. But as the time came for writing it, I knew I wanted to save their marriage. I'm so glad I was able to do that.

Marriage isn't always fairy tale happily-ever-after. To have a long, healthy marriage, good communication is key. Brad and Francie were doing a rotten job of keeping in touch with each other, even though they lived in the same house. I have an idea that in the future, that won't happen again. What do you think?

I always love to hear from readers. You can email me through the contact box on my website: www.magdalenascott.com.

I also send a monthly-*ish* newsletter. To sign up for that, enter your email in the form on this page: http://www.magdalenascott.com/p/contact.html

Until we meet again—Happy Reading!

Magdalena

For Free Reads, Sneak Previews & backstage info, become a Newsletter Subscriber!

I love to connect with readers! Please sign up for my newsletter so we can stay in touch. Don't worry about me clogging up your email inbox—I only send an email if I have actual news to share. The sign-up form is on my website. Just type into your browser: http://www.magdalenascott.com/p/contact.html

Also in the Serendipity, Indiana series

SMALL TOWN CHRISTMAS

Melissa is moving back to Serendipity, Indiana to raise her young son and run her new business—in spite of a painful past and the fact that her ex-boyfriend still lives in their hometown.

EMILY'S DREAMS

Emily Kincaid has a second chance at life, and a voice in her head that keeps nudging her along. But she can't move forward without dealing with her past.

CHRISTMAS WEDDING

Dec. 1: Jim Standish is ready—right this minute—to marry the love of his life, but Melissa Singer wants the day to be one they'll look back on forever. Planning and execution time: 25 days. Will it be possible to create the perfect Christmas Wedding?

THE BLANK BOOK

Alice Williams is surviving widowhood, but must unlock the secrets of a mysterious blank book before she can confidently step into her future with a man she's afraid to love.

THE RING

Happily-ever-after is out of the question. But in Serendipity, the Magic of Love does amazing things.

THE ROAD NOT TAKEN

Francie Standish Carrington has some tough decisions to make, and a lot of questions about a past she thought she understood.

A PIECE OF HER SOUL

Jacqueline needs a break from the constant strain of the special gift she has. But the little cottage on a quiet street isn't quite the retreat she expected, due to the presence of a handsome next door neighbor.

ONCE UPON A TIME

Taylor Kincaid has big plans for her life, and falling in love with the mysterious new shop owner in her hometown isn't one of them. Sweet romance, "coincidences" that might be more than that, and a love that survives the unthinkable come together in this new Serendipity, Indiana tale.

A COWBOY FOR CHRISTMAS

Hannah Kincaid has her eye on Jacob Hollingsworth, the handsome co-owner of Serendipity's new (and only) dude ranch. When Jacob's brother Michael shows up, everything at the Rocking H is turned on its head-- including Hannah's plans.

Magdalena's Legend, Tennessee Titles

MIDNIGHT IN LEGEND, TN

CHRISTMAS COLLISION

WHERE HER HEART IS

BUILDING A DREAM

SECOND CHANCES

CHRISTMAS CHARM

HOME FOR CHRISTMAS

UNDER THE MISTLETOE (Prequel)

THE HOLLY AND THE IVY (Prequel)

A Piece of Her Soul

Serendipity, Indiana—Book 7

Copyright, Magdalena Scott

A Piece of Her Soul—Chapter One

"MOTHER FELL DOWN her basement steps. She's going to be okay. I just wanted you to know."

I'd been fixing dinner in my RV, but at my sister's words, all the air left my lungs. I shut off the gas burner, and collapsed into a captain's chair with my cell in hand. The chair started to spin.

"She's going to be okay—as in, she has broken bones that will mend? What?" I know my tone was less than sweet, but I'd been blindsided by Jen's news.

"Yes, that. One bone in her leg. And lots of bruises. She's in the hospital, and after that it's a rehab place, and then... Well, we're not sure yet. Marcus and I have discussed it—"

"You've discussed it with Mother, too, right?" Jen and her husband would try to do the best thing for

Mother. But she should make the decision for herself, if possible.

"Mother's not really able to talk about it now, Jacquie. She isn't herself yet. The meds." Jen sounded exhausted.

That's all I needed to hear. Mother had always been a rock—for many people, but particularly for me, the wayward daughter. When she got out of rehab, she'd be eager to get back to the home she loved, that she and Dad had built. If I could make it an easy, safe option, that's what I needed to do.

Until this accident she had been busy and vibrant, taking trips or doing projects with her best buddy, Lillian Standish. She made meals and delivered to folks who were ill or bereaved, volunteered at a couple of nonprofits in town, participated in at least one book club... I didn't know all of it, but I knew Mother wouldn't be ready to give up—or at least shouldn't be.

"Jen, I'm coming. I'll get out of here as quickly as possible, and start driving. When will she be released from rehab?"

"Around the first of October, the doctor says."

Her voice was strained. Did Jen doubt my sincerity after such a long absence?

Resolved, I made a mental inventory of the tasks I'd need to finish, avoiding a close scan of my paper calendar. My cat, Sam, jumped onto my lap, demanding to be stroked.

"October first," I repeated. "I can make that work. I'll be in Serendipity, stay with her so she can go home. At least—assuming you don't have a problem with that idea? I know you and Marcus have stuff going on, and I can be flexible."

I could *learn* to be, right? Flexibility was something I had always admired in others, though my version of it tended to be driven by a need to get *away* from a situation, not step *into* one. "Don't you think she'll do better in familiar surroundings?"

There was a long moment of silence. Then, "Yes, I do, and I was trying to figure out how to make it happen. I think you're right about coming home—it would be great medicine for her. You know how she feels about that house. I'm sure she'd love to have you with her, Jacquie." She paused again. "This is very generous. Umm... I'll let you surprise her when you get here."

Meaning, Jen wasn't sure quite I'd come through on the promise. I couldn't blame her for being cautious. If Mother got excited about me returning so she could be home, and then I didn't show up, that would stink, and Jen would be left playing clean-up.

I summoned a light tone. "Perfect, Jen. I love the idea of being a happy surprise for once. Thanks for calling. It means a lot that you thought of me, and let me know right away. Keep me updated, okay?"

"Yes. Sure, I will. And of course I thought of you. I think of you a lot, Jacquie. Miss you." I could imagine the look on her face. A little bit dazed by my stated intention. By the possibility of the absent sister showing up and doing the right thing.

If she only knew about my relationship with doing the right thing. She was better off thinking whatever she did about me.

"Great. If there's nothing else, I need to run for now, Jen."

But the truth was, I didn't need to run. I'd been

running for years, and it was time to do the opposite. I had felt pulled toward Serendipity for a while, and now there was no putting it off. I hoped I was strong enough to do what would be required of me there.

****

There was no doubt that the gossip tree of little Serendipity, Indiana would start buzzing with news of my reappearance, as soon as someone recognized me. I couldn't let myself care. My purpose wasn't to impress anyone or win a popularity contest, but to help Mother, and Jen.

On the other hand, what *I* needed right now was a nice, quiet cave to hide in. A cave that wasn't cold, damp, or dark, but well-lit and airy, with a lovely view of... Okay, not a cave. I could make do with an out-of-the-way camping spot for my RV van, with no close neighbors, and breathtaking scenery on every side. I needed a place to rest, and to heal.

Unlike Mother's injury, mine was invisible. And I intended to keep it a secret from everyone who wasn't already aware of it. My focus was on Mother, not myself.

To have an extended period of time with her would be a treat, in spite of the reason for it. As long as Mother and I were in her house together, or just around our family, I should be fine. But what about the proximity to so many people I'd known back in the day? I shivered at the possibilities.

A few years ago, in a fit of homesickness, I had considered a visit. I pressed Jen to tell me what people thought of my absence, and she finally conceded to my prodding.

"If you're not going to rest until you know, Jacquie, a lot of the town folks think you're an ungrateful egomaniac."

That hurt, but wasn't a surprise. "Oh, nice. Why did I ask?"

"Mmm-hmm. You know how people are."

"Sad to say, yes I do." The fact that I knew, much too intimately, how people are should have warned me off the question, and off of expecting to ever feel at home again in Serendipity.

Find A PIECE OF HER SOUL at your favorite retailer.